D1147125

This Little Tiger book belongs to:

WALTHAM FOREST LIBRARIES
90400000116812

Toe NAILS
LEECHES
ROTTEN CUSTARD
BELLY BUTTON FLUFF
NAILS
GARLIC TONIC
STINK POWDER
GOOOEY EAR WAX
ROTTEN LEAVES
INSTA MUD
TRUMPING POWDER
Feed Frog
Feed spiders
Add wax
TINY
EXTRA LARGE
NORMAL BOGEYS
SPIDERS.
CAUTION.....

SMELLY POND WATER
WITCH BREW
ITCHING POWDER
JUICY WET EARTH WORMS
SWAMP WATER
DON'T FLUSH TOILET
DON'T CLEAN POTS
DON'T WASH!
SPLASH IN PUDDLES
PLUG HOLE BITS & SLIME
SICK BAG
HAIR
MAGGOTS
FLIES
YUMMY!
BONES
cheese

For Mark, Anna and Charlotte
with my love – T C

To Laura, Grace and Oscar
for putting up with Trolls in the house
– L W

Daily Wail

Little Tiger Press
An imprint of Magi Publications
1 The Coda Centre, 189 Munster Road,
London SW6 6AW • www.littletigerpress.com
First published in Great Britain 2010
This edition published 2010
Text copyright © Tracey Corderoy 2010
Illustrations copyright © Lee Wildish 2010
Tracey Corderoy and Lee Wildish have asserted their rights
to be identified as the author and illustrator of this work
under the Copyright, Designs and Patents Act, 1988
A CIP catalogue record for this book is available
from the British Library • All rights reserved
ISBN 978-1-84895-051-1 • Printed in Singapore
10 9 8 7 6 5 4 3 2 1

WALTHAM FOREST
90400000116812
PETERS | 10-May-2011
£5.99 | JF
M

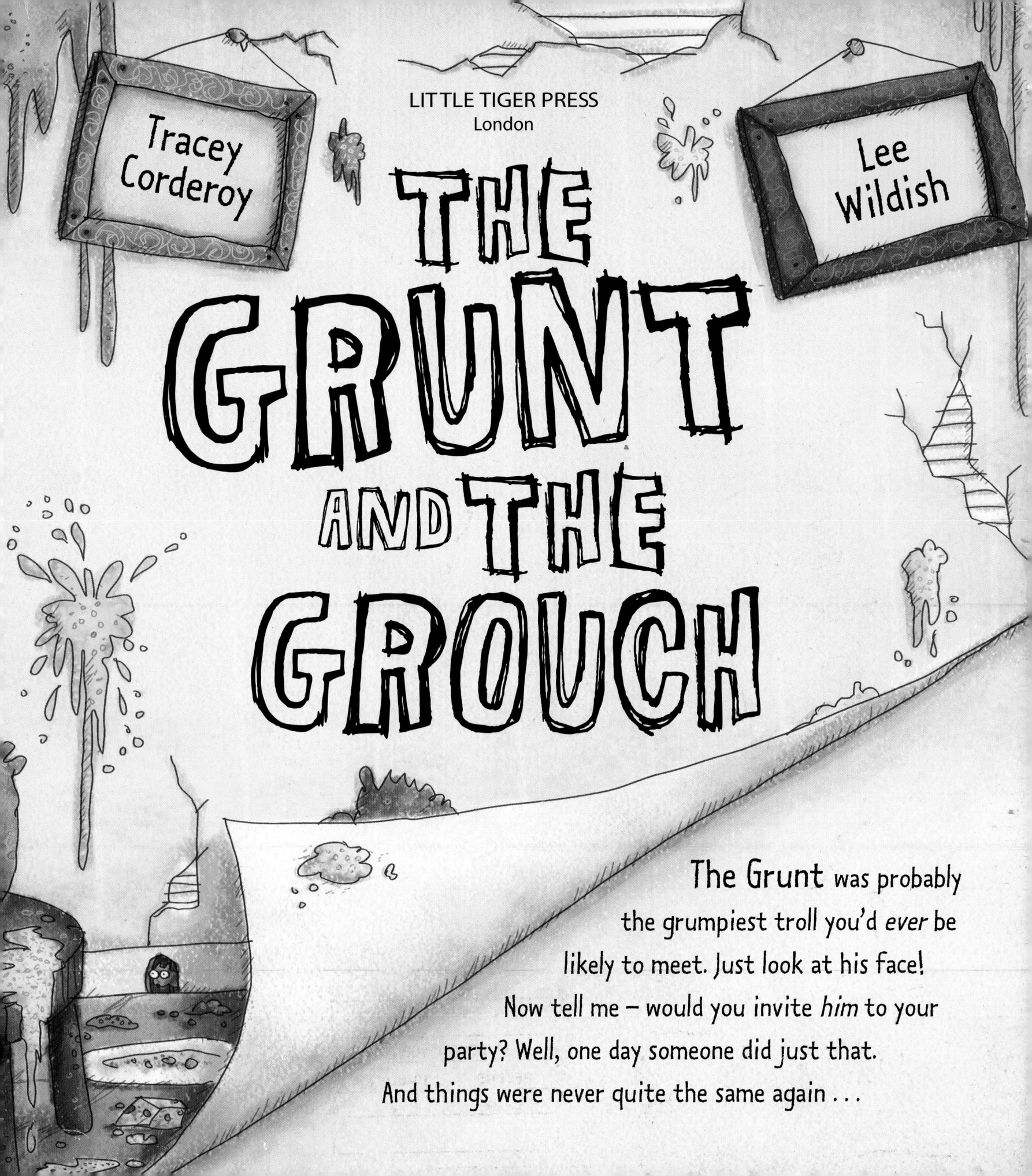
Tracey Corderoy
Lee Wildish
LITTLE TIGER PRESS
London
THE GRUNT AND THE GROUCH
The Grunt was probably the grumpiest troll you'd *ever* be likely to meet. Just look at his face! Now tell me – would you invite *him* to your party? Well, one day someone did just that. And things were never quite the same again . . .

It happened on a Tuesday – the most *boring* day of the week –
this scrappy bit of paper landed on The Grunt's dirty doormat . . .
"What's **this?**" he cried, snatching it up.
So he read the scruffy writing . . .

Dear Neighbour,
I'm having a party.
And - guess what?
You're invited!
There'll be stuff
to eat and everything.
PS. Don't forget
my pressie.

"Who's **dared** leave this on my mat?"
growled The Grunt.
"I **don't** like Tuesdays. I **don't** like visitors.
And I **really don't** like parties . . .
so I'm not coming!"

With that, he tore the invitation
into tiny shreds, then stomped back
inside and finally got to work . . .

Boring Tuesday morning ended and boring Tuesday afternoon began. So The Grunt went to town – it was, after all, the perfect place . . .

...to be
horrid!

So he **jumped** in
muddy puddles . . .

growled at
kitty cats . . .

and **swiped** a teddy from
every pram he saw!

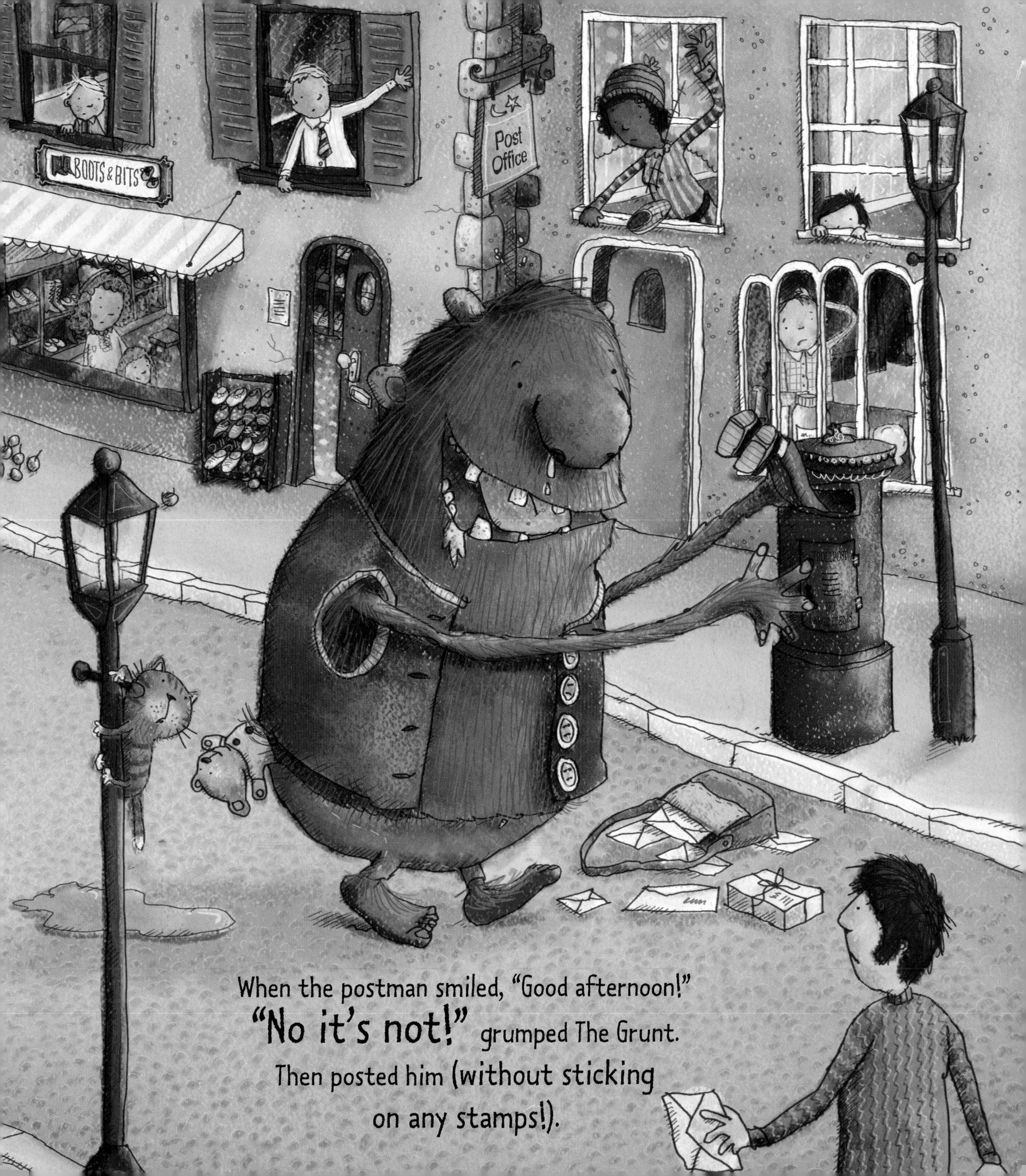

When the postman smiled, "Good afternoon!"
"No it's not!" grumped The Grunt.
Then posted him (without sticking
on any stamps!).

Back home, as The Grunt thundered in through his gate, who should he find but **a visitor!**

"Grrrrrr!" he bellowed. "I'm The Grunt! No one parties in **my** garden!"

He waved a dirty fingernail.
"Now clear off!" he snarled.
Then **bang – bang – bang** went the pretty balloons
as The Grunt popped every one!

"Oi – party pooper!" snapped The Grouch.
"You great big grunty grump!"
Then he chucked a chunk of
his pongiest cheese . . .

And that's when the food

fight began.

"Hang on a minute . . ." said The Grunt.
"Those maggot-cakes look **great!**"
So they sat and ate and The Grunt had such fun
he forgot to be mean . . . he forgot to be *bored* and
he *even* forgot to send The Grouch away!

"Now . . ." burped The Grunt.
"What else can we do?"

"Troll stuff!" cried The Grouch.
So they messed around with spots and goo . . .
SMALL ONES
BIG bogeys
Medium bogeys

took turns to **cheat** at
a game or two . . .

and hid from the sunshine . . .
together!

A whole week later, The Grouch packed up his tent.
"Oh well, Grunty," he sighed. "It's been **great!**
But now I must go. See – I always
move garden on a Tuesday . . ."

"But . . . *why?*" said The Grunt. And then he saw it – the tiny troll looked . . . *sad.* The Grunt had never seen sad before. What's more, he'd never cared! But now . . . suddenly . . . he did.

"You asked me why I go," said The Grouch, disappearing through the gate. "I go because . . . no one's ever asked me to stay."

The Grunt sat and thought, then . . .
"Wait!" he cried, tearing off after his friend.
"Grouchy – hey – come back!" he called.
"It won't be the same without *you!*"

But where was The Grouch?
He'd disappeared! So The Grunt
searched high and low.

He raced. He chased.
He dashed. He crashed!

And then, at last . . .

. . . he **found him!**

"Grouchy – stay!" panted The Grunt.

"Wow – thanks . . ." sniffed the little Grouch.

Then The Grunt felt his lips go all tickly
and begin to curl up to his ears . . .
"What's this?" he said. It felt *so good!*
And The Grouch cried, "I think we're **smiling!**"

Now The Grunt and The Grouch are the **happiest** trolls you'd ever be likely to meet!

Still they **never** pick bits of mould off their teeth...

Never clean the bath...

Never do the washing up...

And never, ever, EVER flush the toilet!

But, every Tuesday, they get dressed up.
Now it's their **favourite** day!
For that's the day . . .

HARPY BIRTHDAY, CECIL
TROLLS RULE!

. . . they PARTY!
(So watch out!)

Toe NAILS
LEECHES
ROTTEN CUSTARD
BELLY BUTTON FLUFF
GARLIC TONIC
STINK POWDER
GOOOEY EAR WAX
ROTTEN LEAVES
INSTA MUD
TRUMPING POWDER
Feed Frog
Feed Spiders
Add wax
TINY
EXTRA LARGE
NORMAL BOGEYS
SPIDERS.
CAUTION.....

SMELLY POND WATER
WITCH BREW
ITCHING POWDER
JUICY WET EARTH WORMS
SWAMP WATER
DON'T FLUSH TOILET
DON'T CLEAN POTS
DON'T WASH!
SPLASH IN PUDDLES
PLUG HOLE BITS & SLIME
ICK
SAG
FLIES
YUMMY!
BONES
cheese
HAIR
MAGGOTS

You'll never be grouchy with these books from Little Tiger Press!
Sylvia and Bird
Catherine Rayner
YUCK! That's not a Monster!
Angela McAllister
Alison Edgson
Rhino's Great BIG Itch!
Natalie Chivers
PAUL BRIGHT
CHARLIE'S SUPERHERO UNDERPANTS
Lee Wildish
The Three Horrid Pigs and the Big Friendly Wolf
by Liz Pichon
Bright Stanley and the Cave Monster
Matt Buckingham
For information regarding any of the above titles or for our catalogue, please contact us:
Little Tiger Press, 1 The Coda Centre, 189 Munster Road, London SW6 6AW
Tel: 020 7385 6333 • Fax: 020 7385 7333 • E-mail: info@littletiger.co.uk • www.littletigerpress.com